HORRID HENRY
AND THE
MUMMY'S CURSE

Francesca Simon spent her childhood on the beach in California, and then went to Yale and Oxford Universities to study medieval history and literature. She now lives in London with her family. She has written over 45 books and won the Children's Book of the Year in 2008 at the Galaxy British Book Awards for *Horrid Henry and the Abominable Snowman*.

Also by Francesca Simon

Don't Cook Cinderella
Helping Hercules

and for younger readers
Don't Be Horrid, Henry

The Topsy-Turvies
Illustrated by Emily Bolam

There is a complete list of **Horrid Henry** titles
at the end of the book.
Horrid Henry is also available on audio CD and
digital download, all read by Miranda Richardson.

Visit Horrid Henry's website at
www.horridhenry.co.uk for competitions,
games, downloads and a monthly newsletter

HORRID HENRY
AND THE
MUMMY'S CURSE

Francesca Simon
Illustrated by Tony Ross

Orion
Children's Books

First published in Great Britain in 2000
by Orion Children's Books
Reissued in paperback 2008
by Orion Children's Books
a division of the Orion Publishing Group Ltd
Orion House
5 Upper Saint Martin's Lane
London WC2H 9EA
An Hachette Livre UK Company

5 7 9 10 8 6

Text © Francesca Simon 2000
Illustrations © Tony Ross 2000

The moral right of Francesca Simon and Tony Ross
to be identified as author and illustrator
of this work has been asserted.

The Orion Publishing Group's policy is to use papers that are natural,
renewable and recyclable products and made from wood grown in
sustainable forests. The logging and manufacturing processes are expected to
conform to the environmental regulations of the country of origin.

A catalogue record for this book is available from the British Library.

Printed in Great Britain by Clays Ltd, St Ives plc

ISBN 978 1 85881 824 5

www.horridhenry.co.uk
www.orionbooks.co.uk

For my friends and advisers,
Joe and Freddy Gaminara

CONTENTS

1 Horrid Henry's Hobby   9

2 Horrid Henry's Homework   29

3 Horrid Henry's Swimming Lesson   49

4 Horrid Henry and the
  Mummy's Curse   67

1

HORRID HENRY'S HOBBY

"Out of my way, worm!" shrieked Horrid Henry, pushing past his younger brother Perfect Peter and dashing into the kitchen.

"NO!" screamed Perfect Peter. He scrambled after Henry and clutched his leg.

"Get off me!" shouted Henry. He grabbed the unopened Sweet Tweet cereal box. "Nah nah ne nah nah, I got it first."

Perfect Peter lunged for the Sweet Tweet box and snatched it from Henry. "But it's my turn!"

"No, mine!" shrieked Henry.

He ripped open the top and stuck his hand inside.

"It's mine!" shrieked Peter. He ripped open the bottom.

A small wrapped toy fell to the floor.

Henry and Peter both lunged for it.

"Gimme that!" yelled Henry.

"But it's my turn to have it!" yelled Peter.

"Stop being horrid, Henry!" shouted Mum. "Now give me that thing!"

Henry and Peter both held on tight.

10

"NO!" screamed Henry and Peter. "IT'S MY TURN TO HAVE THE TOY!"

Horrid Henry and Perfect Peter both collected Gizmos from inside Sweet Tweet cereal boxes. So did everyone at their school. There were ten different coloured Gizmos to collect, from the common green to the rare gold. Both Henry and Peter had Gizmos of every colour. Except for one. Gold.

11

"Right," said Mum, "whose turn is it to get the toy?"

"MINE!" screamed Henry and Peter.

"He got the last one!" screeched Henry. "Remember – he opened the new box and got the blue Gizmo."

It was true that Perfect Peter had got the blue Gizmo – two boxes ago. But why should Peter get any? If he hadn't started collecting Gizmos to copy me, thought Henry resentfully, I'd get every single one.

"NO!" howled Peter. He burst into tears. "Henry opened the last box."

"Cry-baby," jeered Henry.

"Stop it," said Peter.

"Stop it," mimicked Henry.

"Mum, Henry's teasing me," wailed Peter.

"I remember now," said Mum. "It's Peter's turn."

12

"Thank you, Mum," said Perfect Peter.

"It's not fair!" screamed Horrid Henry
as Peter tore open the wrapping. There
was a gold gleam.

"Oh my goodness," gasped Peter.
"A gold Gizmo!"

Horrid Henry felt as if he'd been
punched in the stomach. He stared at the
glorious, glowing, golden Gizmo.

"It's not fair!" howled Henry. "I want a
gold Gizmo!"

"I'm sorry, Henry," said Mum. "It'll be
your turn next."

"But I want the gold one!" screamed Henry.

He leaped on Peter and yanked the Gizmo out of his hand. He was Hurricane Henry uprooting everything in his path.

"Helllllllllp!" howled Peter.

"Stop being horrid, Henry, or no more Gizmos for you!" shouted Mum. "Now clean up this mess and get dressed."

"NO!" howled Henry. He ran upstairs to his room, slamming the door behind him.

He had to have a gold Gizmo. He simply had to. No one at school had a gold one. Henry could see himself now, the centre of attention, everyone pushing and shoving just to get a look at his gold Gizmo. Henry could charge 20p a peek. Everyone would want to see it and to hold it. Henry would be invited to every birthday party. Instead, Peter would be the star attraction. Henry gnashed his teeth just thinking about it.

But how could he get one? You couldn't buy Gizmos. You could only get them inside Sweet Tweet cereal boxes. Mum was so mean she made Henry and Peter finish the old box before she'd buy a new one. Henry had eaten mountains of Sweet Tweet cereal to collect all his Gizmos. All that hard work would be in vain, unless he got a gold one.

He could, of course, steal Peter's. But

Peter would be sure to notice, and Henry would be the chief suspect.

He could swap. Yes! He would offer Peter *two* greens! That was generous. In fact, that was really generous. But Peter hated doing swaps. For some reason he always thought Henry was trying to cheat him.

And then suddenly Henry had a brilliant, spectacular idea. True, it did involve a little tiny teensy weensy bit of trickery, but Henry's cause was just. *He'd* been collecting Gizmos far longer than Peter had. He deserved a gold one, and Peter didn't.

"So, you got a gold Gizmo," said Henry, popping into Peter's room. "I'm really sorry."

Perfect Peter looked up from polishing his Gizmos. "Why?" he said suspiciously. "*Everyone* wants a gold Gizmo."

16

Horrid Henry looked sadly at Perfect
Peter. "Not any more. They're very
unlucky, you know. Every single person
who's got one has died horribly."

Perfect Peter stared at Henry, then at
his golden Gizmo.

"That's not true, Henry."

"Yes it is."

"No it isn't."

Horrid Henry walked slowly around
Peter's room. Every so often he made a
little note in a notebook.

"Marbles, check. Three knights, check.
Nature kit – nah. Coin collection,
check."

"What are you doing?" said Peter.

"Just looking round your stuff to
see what I want when you're gone."

"Stop it!" said Peter. "You just made
that up about gold Gizmos – didn't
you?"

17

"No," said Henry. "It's in all the news-
papers. There was the boy out walking his
dog who fell into a pit of molten lava.

There was the girl who drowned in the
loo, and then that poor boy who—"

"I don't want to die," said Perfect
Peter. He looked pale. "What am I going
to do?"

Henry paused. "There's nothing you
can do. Once you've got it you're sunk."

Peter jumped up.

"I'll throw it away!"

"That wouldn't work," said Henry. "You'd still be jinxed. There's only one way out—"

"What?" said Perfect Peter.

"If you give the gold away to someone brave enough to take it, then the jinx passes to them."

"But no one will take it from me!" wailed Peter.

"Tell you what," said Henry. "I'll take the risk."

"Are you sure?" said Peter.

"Of course," said Horrid Henry. "You're my brother. You'd risk your life for me."

"OK," said Peter. He handed Henry the gold Gizmo. "Thank you, Henry. You're the best brother in the world."

"I know," said Horrid Henry.

He actually had his very own gold

Gizmo in his hand. It was his, fair and square. He couldn't wait to see Moody Margaret's face when he waved it in front of her. And Rude Ralph. He would be green with envy.

Then Perfect Peter burst into tears and ran downstairs.

"Mum!" he wailed. "Henry's going to die! And it's all my fault."

"What?" screeched Mum.

Uh oh, thought Henry. He clutched his treasure.

Mum stormed upstairs. She snatched the gold Gizmo from Henry.

"How could you be so horrid, Henry?" shouted Mum. "No TV for a week! Poor Peter. Now get ready. We're going shopping."

"NO!" howled Henry. "I'm not going!"

Horrid Henry scowled as he followed
Mum up and down the aisles of the
Happy Shopper. He'd crashed the cart
into some people so Mum wouldn't let
him push it. Then she caught him
filling the cart with crisps and fizzy
drinks and made him put them all back.
What a horrible rotten day this had
turned out to be.

21

"Yum, cabbage," said Perfect Peter. "Could we get some?"

"Certainly," said Mum.

"And spinach, my favourite!" said Peter.

"Help yourself," said Mum.

"I want sweets!" screamed Henry.

"No," said Mum.

"I want doughnuts!" screamed Henry.

"No!" screamed Mum.

"There's nothing to eat here!" shrieked Henry.

"Stop being horrid, Henry," hissed Mum. "Everyone's looking."

"I don't care."

"Well I do," said Mum. "Now make yourself useful. Go and get a box of Sweet Tweets."

"All right," said Henry. Now was his chance to escape. Before Mum could stop him he grabbed a cart and

whizzed off.

"Watch out for the racing driver!" squealed Henry. Shoppers scattered as he zoomed down the aisle and screeched to a halt in front of the cereal section. There were the Sweet Tweets. A huge pile of them, in a display tower, under a twinkling sign saying, "A free Gizmo in every box! Collect them all!"

Henry reached for a box and put it in his cart.

And then Horrid Henry stopped. What was the point of buying a whole box if it just contained another green Gizmo? Henry didn't think he could bear it. I'll just check what's inside, he thought. Then, if it *is* a green one, I'll be prepared for the disappointment.

Carefully, he opened the box and slipped his hand inside. Aha! There was the toy. He lifted it out, and held it up to the light. Rats! A green Gizmo, just what he'd feared.

But wait. There was bound to be a child out there longing for a green Gizmo to complete his collection just as much as Henry was longing for a gold. Wouldn't it be selfish and horrid of Henry to take a green he didn't need when it would make someone else so happy?

I'll just peek inside one more box,

24

thought Horrid Henry, replacing the box
he'd opened and reaching for another.

Rip! He tore it open. Red.

Hmmm, thought Henry. Red is
surplus to requirements.

Rip! Another box opened. Blue.

Rip! Rip! Rip!

Green! Green! Blue!

I'll just try one more at the back, thought Henry. He stood on tiptoe, and stretched as far as he could. His hand reached inside the box and grabbed hold of the toy.

The tower wobbled.

CRASH!

Horrid Henry sprawled on the ground. Henry was covered in Sweet Tweets. So was the floor. So were all the shoppers.

"HELP!" screamed the manager, skidding in the mess. "Whose horrid boy is this?"

There was a very long silence.

"Mine," whispered Mum.

Horrid Henry sat in the kitchen surrounded by boxes and boxes and boxes of Sweet Tweets. He'd be eating Sweet Tweets for breakfast, lunch and dinner for weeks. But it was worth it, thought Henry happily. Banned for life from the Happy Shopper, how wonderful. He uncurled his hand to enjoy again the glint of gold.

Although he *had* noticed that Scrummy Yummies were offering a free Twizzle card in every box. Hmmmm, Twizzle cards.

27

2

HORRID HENRY'S HOMEWORK

Ahhhh, thought Horrid Henry. He turned on the TV and stretched out. School was over. What could be better than lying on the sofa all afternoon, eating crisps and watching TV? Wasn't life grand?

Then Mum came in. She did not look like a mum who thought life was grand. She looked like a mum on the warpath against boys who lay on sofas all afternoon, eating crisps and watching TV.

"Get your feet off the sofa, Henry!" said Mum.

"Unh," grunted Henry.

"Stop getting crisps everywhere!" snapped Mum.

"Unh," grunted Henry.

"Have you done your homework, Henry?" said Mum.

Henry didn't answer.

"HENRY!" shouted Mum.

"WHAT!" shouted Henry.

"Have you done your homework?"

"What homework?" said Henry. He kept his eyes glued to the TV.

"Go, Mutants!" he screeched.

"The five spelling words you are meant to learn tonight," said Mum.

"Oh," said Henry. "*That* homework."

Horrid Henry hated homework. He had far better things to do with his precious time than learn how to spell "zipper" or work out the answer to 6 x 7. For weeks Henry's homework sheets had ended up in the recycling box until Dad found them. Henry swore he had no idea how they got there and blamed

30

Fluffy the cat, but since then Mum and Dad had checked his school bag every day.

Mum snatched the zapper and switched off the telly.

"Hey, I'm watching!" said Henry.

"When are you going to do your homework, Henry?" said Mum.

"SOON!" screamed Henry. He'd just returned from a long, hard day at school. Couldn't he have any peace around here? When he was king anyone who said the word "homework" would get thrown to the crocodiles.

"I had a phone call today from Miss Battle-Axe," said Mum. "She said you got a zero in the last ten spelling tests."

"That's not *my* fault," said Henry. "First I lost the words, then I forgot, then I couldn't read my writing, then I copied the words wrong, then—"

"I don't want to hear any more silly excuses," said Mum. "Do you know your spelling words for tomorrow?"

"Yes," lied Henry.

"Where's the list?" Mum asked.

"I don't know," said Henry.

"Find it or no TV for a month," said Mum.

"It's not fair," muttered Henry, digging the crumpled spelling list out of his pocket.

Mum looked at it.

"There's going to be a test tomorrow," she said. "How do you spell 'goat'?"

32

"Don't you know how, Mum?" asked
Henry.

"Henry. . ." said Mum.

Henry scowled.

"I'm busy," moaned Henry. "I promise
I'll tell you right after Mutant Madman.
It's my favourite show."

"How do you spell 'goat'?" said Mum.

"G-O-T-E," snapped Henry.

"Wrong," said Mum. "What about
'boat'?"

"Why do I have to do this?" wailed
Henry.

"Because it's your homework," said
Mum. "You have to learn how to spell."

"But why?" said Henry. "I never write
letters."

"Because," said Mum. "Now spell
"boat".

"B-O-T-T-E," said Henry.

"No more TV until you do your

33

homework," said Mum.

"I've done all *my* homework," said
Perfect Peter. "In fact I enjoyed it so much
I've already done tomorrow's homework
as well."

Henry pounced on Peter. He was a
cannibal tenderising his victim for the pot.

"Eeeeyowwwww!" screamed Peter.

"Henry! Go to your room!" shouted
Mum. "And don't come out until you
know *all* your spelling words!"

Horrid Henry stomped upstairs and

slammed his bedroom door. This was so unfair! He was far too busy to bother with stupid, boring, useless spelling. For instance, he hadn't read the new Mutant Madman comic book. He hadn't finished drawing that treasure map. And he hadn't even begun to sort his new collection of Twizzle cards. Homework would have to wait.

There was just one problem. Miss Battle-Axe had said that everyone who spelled all their words correctly tomorrow would get a pack of Big Bopper sweets. Henry loved Big Bopper sweets. Mum and Dad hardly ever let him have them. But why on earth did he have to learn spelling words to get some? If *he* were the teacher, he'd only give sweets to children who couldn't spell. Henry sighed. He'd just have to sit down and learn those stupid words.

4:30. Mum burst into the room. Henry was lying on his bed reading a comic.

"Henry! Why aren't you doing your homework?" said Mum.

"I'll do it in a sec'," said Henry. "I'm just finishing this page."

"Henry..." said Mum.

Henry put down the comic.

Mum left. Henry picked up the comic.

5.30. Dad burst into the room. Henry was playing with his knights.

"Henry! Why aren't you doing your homework?" said Dad.

"I'm tired!" yawned Henry. "I'm just taking a little break. It's hard having so much work!"

"Henry, you've only got five words to learn!" said Dad. "And you've just spent two hours *not* learning them."

"All right," snarled Henry. Slowly, he picked up his spelling list. Then he put it down again. He had to get in the mood. Soothing music, that's what he needed. Horrid Henry switched on his cassette player. The terrible sound of the Driller Cannibals boomed through the house.

"OH, I'M A CAN-CAN-CANNI-BAL!" screamed Henry, stomping around his room. "DON'T CALL ME AN ANIMAL JUST 'CAUSE I'M A CAN-CAN-CANNIBAL!"

Mum and Dad stormed into Henry's bedroom and turned off the music.

"That's enough, Henry!" said Dad.

"DO YOUR HOMEWORK!" screamed Mum.

"IF YOU DON'T GET EVERY SINGLE WORD RIGHT IN YOUR TEST TOMORROW THERE WILL

BE NO TELEVISION FOR A WEEK!"
shouted Dad.

EEEK! No TV *and* no sweets! This was
too much. Horrid Henry looked at his
spelling words with loathing.

GOAT
BOAT
SAID
STOAT
FRIEND

"I hate goats! I'll never need to spell
the word 'goat' in my life," said Henry.
He hated goat's cheese. He hated goat's
milk. He thought goats were smelly. That

was one word he'd definitely never need to know.

The next word was "boat". Who needs to spell that, thought Henry. I'm not going to be a sailor when I grow up. I get seasick. In fact, it's bad for my health to learn how to spell 'boat'.

As for "said", what did it matter if he spelt it "sed"? It was perfectly understandable, written "sed." Only an old fusspot like Miss Battle-Axe would mind such a tiny mistake.

Then there was "stoat". What on earth was a stoat? What a mean, sneaky word. Henry wouldn't know a stoat if it sat on him. Of all the useless, horrible words, "stoat" was the worst. Trust his teacher, Miss Battle-Axe, to make him learn a horrible, useless word like stoat.

The last word was "friend". Well, a real friend like Rude Ralph didn't care how the word "friend" was spelt. As far as Henry was concerned any friend who minded how he spelt "friend" was no friend. Miss Battle-Axe included that word to torture him.

Five whole spelling words. It was too much. I'll never learn so many words, thought Henry. But what about tomorrow? He'd have to watch Moody Margaret and Jolly Josh and Clever Clare chomping away at those delicious Big Boppers, while he, Henry, had to gnash his empty teeth. Plus no TV for a week! Henry couldn't live that long without TV! He was sunk. He was doomed to be sweetless, and TV-less.

But wait. What if there was a way to get those sweets without the horrid hassle of learning to spell? Suddenly, Henry had a brilliant, spectacular idea. It was so simple Henry couldn't believe he'd never thought of it before.

He sat next to Clever Clare. Clare always knew the spelling words. All Henry had to do was to take a little peek at her work. If he positioned his chair right, he'd easily be able to see what she wrote. And he wouldn't be copying her, no way. Just double-checking. I am a genius, thought Horrid Henry. 100% right on the test. Loads of Big Bopper sweets. Mum and Dad would be so thrilled they'd let him watch extra TV. Hurray!

Horrid Henry swaggered into class the next morning. He sat down in his seat between Clever Clare and Beefy Bert. Carefully, he inched his chair over a fraction so that he had a good view of Clare's paper.

"Spelling test!" barked Miss Battle-Axe. "First word – goat."

Clare bent over her paper. Henry pretended he was staring at the wall, then, quick as a flash, he glanced at her work and wrote "goat".

"Boat," said Miss Battle-Axe. Again Horrid Henry sneaked a look at Clare's paper and copied her. And again.

43

And again.

This is fantastic, thought Henry. I'll never have to learn any spelling words. Just think of all the comic books he could read instead of wasting his time on homework! He sneaked a peek at Beefy Bert's paper. Blank. Ha ha, thought Henry.

There was only one word left. Henry could taste the tingly tang of a Big Bopper already. Wouldn't he swagger about! And no way would he share his sweets with anyone.

Suddenly, Clare shifted position and edged away from him. Rats! Henry couldn't see her paper any more.

"Last word," boomed Miss Battle-Axe. "Friend."

Henry twisted in his seat. He could see the first four words. He just needed to get a tiny bit closer . . .

Clare looked at him. Henry stared at the ceiling. Clare glared, then looked back at her paper. Quickly, Henry leaned over and . . . YES! He copied down the final word, "friend".

Victory!

Chomp! Chomp! Chomp! Hmmnn, boy, did those Big Boppers taste great!

Someone tapped him on the shoulder. It was Miss Battle-Axe. She was smiling at him with her great big yellow teeth.

45

Miss Battle-Axe had never smiled at Henry before.

"Well, Henry," said Miss Battle-Axe. "What an improvement! I'm thrilled."

"Thank you," said Henry modestly.

"In fact, you've done so well I'm promoting you to the top spelling group. Twenty-five extra words a night. Here's the list."

Horrid Henry's jaws stopped chomping. He looked in horror at the new spelling list. It was littered with words. But not just any words. Awful words. Mean words. Long words. HARD words.

Hieroglyphs.

Trapezium.

Diarrhoea.

"AAAAAHHHHHHHHHHH!" shrieked Horrid Henry.

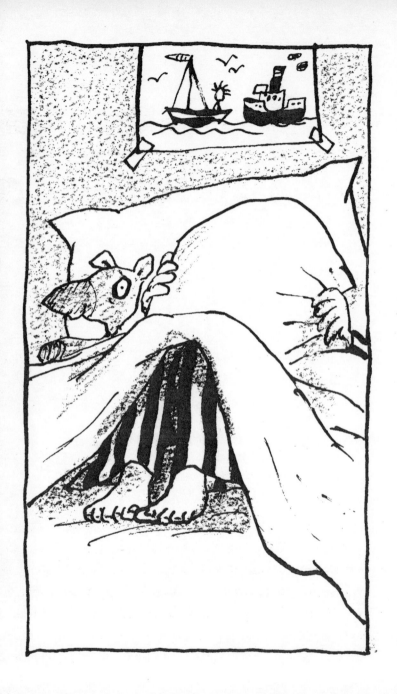

3

HORRID HENRY'S SWIMMING LESSON

Oh no! thought Horrid Henry. He pulled the duvet tightly over his head. It was Thursday. Horrible, horrible, Thursday. The worst day of the week. Horrid Henry was certain Thursdays came more often than any other day.

Thursday was his class swimming day. Henry had a nagging feeling that this Thursday was even worse than all the other awful Thursdays.

49

Horrid Henry liked the bus ride to the pool. Horrid Henry liked doing the dance of the seven towels in the changing room. He also liked hiding in the lockers, throwing socks in the pool, and splashing everyone.

The only thing Henry didn't like

about going swimming was . . . swimming.

The truth was, Horrid Henry hated
water. Ugggh! Water was so . . . wet! And
soggy. The chlorine stung his eyes. He
never knew what horrors might be lurk-
ing in the deep end. And the pool was so
cold penguins could fly in for the winter.

Fortunately, Henry had a brilliant list
of excuses. He'd pretend he had a
verucca, or a tummy ache, or had lost
his swimming costume. Unfortunately,
the mean, nasty, horrible swimming
teacher, Soggy Sid, usually made him
get in the pool anyway.

Then Henry would duck Dizzy Dave,
or splash Weepy William, or pinch
Gorgeous Gurinder, until Sid ordered
him out. It was not surprising that
Horrid Henry had never managed to
get his five-metre badge.

Arrrgh! Now he remembered. Today was test day. The terrible day when everyone had to show how far they could swim. Aerobic Al was going for gold. Moody Margaret was going for silver. The only ones who were still trying for their five-metre badges were Lazy Linda and Horrid Henry. Five whole metres! How could anyone swim such a vast distance?

If only they were tested on who could sink to the bottom of the pool the fastest, or splash the most, or spit water the furthest, then Horrid Henry would have every badge in a jiffy. But no. He had to leap into a freezing cold pool, and, if he survived that shock, somehow thrash his way across five whole metres without drowning.

Well, there was no way he was going to school today.

Mum came into his room.

"I can't go to school today, Mum," Henry moaned. "I feel terrible."

Mum didn't even look at him.

"Thursday-itis again, I presume," said Mum.

"No way!" said Henry. "I didn't even know it was Thursday."

"Get up Henry," said Mum. "You're going swimming and that's that."

Perfect Peter peeked round the door.

"It's badge day today!" he said. "I'm going for 50 metres!"

"That's brilliant, Peter," said Mum. "I bet you're the best swimmer in your class."

Perfect Peter smiled modestly.

"I just try my best," he said. "Good luck with your five-metre badge, Henry," he added.

Horrid Henry growled and attacked.

He was a Venus flytrap slowly mashing a frantic fly between his deadly leaves.

"Eeeeeowwww!" screeched Peter.

"Stop being horrid, Henry!" screamed Mum. "Leave your poor brother alone!"

Horrid Henry let Peter go. If only he could find some way not to take his swimming test he'd be the happiest boy in the world.

Henry's class arrived at the pool. Right, thought Henry. Time to unpack his excuses to Soggy Sid.

"I can't go swimming, I've got a verucca," lied Henry.

"Take off your sock," ordered Soggy Sid.

Rats, thought Henry.

"Maybe it's better now," said Henry.

"I thought so," said Sid.

Horrid Henry grabbed his stomach.

"Tummy pains!" he moaned. "I feel terrible."

"You seemed fine when you were prancing round the pool a moment ago," snapped Sid. "Now get changed."

Time for the killer excuse.

"I forgot my swimming costume!" said Henry. This was his best chance of success.

"No problem," said Soggy Sid. He handed Henry a bag. "Put on one of these."

Slowly, Horrid Henry rummaged in

the bag. He pulled out a bikini top, a blue costume with a hole in the middle, a pair of pink pants, a tiny pair of green trunks, a polka-dot one piece with bunnies, see-through white shorts, and a nappy.

"I can't wear any of these!" protested Horrid Henry.

"You can and you will, if I have to put them on you myself," snarled Sid.

Horrid Henry squeezed into the green

trunks. He could barely breathe. Slowly, he joined the rest of his class pushing and shoving by the side of the pool.

Everyone had millions of badges sewn all over their costumes. You couldn't even see Aerobic Al's bathing suit beneath the stack of badges.

"Hey you!" shouted Soggy Sid. He pointed at Weepy William. "Where's your swimming costume?"

Weepy William glanced down and burst into tears.

"Waaaaah," he wailed, and ran weeping back to the changing room.

"Now get in!" ordered Soggy Sid.

"But I'll drown!" screamed Henry. "I can't swim!"

"Get in!" screamed Soggy Sid.

Goodbye, cruel world. Horrid Henry held his breath and fell into the icy water. ARRRRGH! He was turning into an iceberg!

He was dying! He was dead! His feet flailed madly as he sank down, down, down – clunk! Henry's feet touched the bottom.

Henry stood up, choking and spluttering. He was waist-deep in water.

"Linda and Henry! Swim five metres – now!"

What am I going to do? thought Henry. It was so humiliating not even being able to swim five metres! Everyone would tease him. And he'd have to listen to them bragging about their badges! Wouldn't it be great to get a badge? Somehow?

Lazy Linda set off, very very slowly. Horrid Henry grabbed on to her leg. Maybe she'll pull me across, he thought.

"Ugggh!" gurgled Lazy Linda.

"Leave her alone!" shouted Sid. "Last

58

chance, Henry."

Horrid Henry ran along the pool's
bottom and flapped his arms, pretending
to swim.

"Did it!" said Henry.

Soggy Sid scowled.

"I said swim, not walk!" screamed Sid.
"You've failed. Now get over to the far
lane and practise. Remember, anyone
who stops swimming during the test
doesn't get a badge."

Horrid Henry stomped over to the far
lane. No way was he going to practise!

How he hated swimming! He watched
the others splashing up and down, up and
down. There was Aerobic Al, doing his
laps like a bolt of lightning. And Moody
Margaret. And Kung-Fu Kate. Everyone
would be getting a badge but Henry.
It was so unfair.

"Pssst, Susan," said Henry. "Have you
heard? There's a shark in the deep end!"

"Oh yeah, right," said Sour Susan. She
looked at the dark water in the far end of
the pool.

"Don't believe me," said Henry. "Find

out the hard way. Come back with a leg missing."

Sour Susan paused and whispered something to Moody Margaret.

"Shut up, Henry," said Margaret. They swam off.

"Don't worry about the shark, Andrew," said Henry. "I think he's already eaten today."

"What shark?" said Anxious Andrew.

Andrew stared at the deep end. It did look awfully dark down there.

"Start swimming, Andrew!" shouted Soggy Sid.

"I don't want to," said Andrew.

"Swim! Or I'll bite you myself!" snarled Sid.

Andrew started swimming.

"Dave, Ralph, Clare, and Bert – start swimming!" bellowed Soggy Sid.

"Look out for the shark!" said Horrid

Henry. He watched Aerobic Al tearing up and down the lane. "Gotta swim, gotta swim, gotta swim," muttered Al between strokes.

What a show-off, thought Henry. Wouldn't it be fun to play a trick on him?

Horrid Henry pretended he was a crocodile. He sneaked under the water to the middle of the pool and waited until Aerobic Al swam overhead. Then Horrid Henry reached up.

Pinch! Henry grabbed Al's thrashing leg.

"AAAARGGG!" screamed Al. "Something's grabbed my leg. Help!" Aerobic Al leaped out of the pool.

Tee hee, thought Horrid Henry.

"It's a shark!" screamed Sour Susan. She scrambled out of the pool.

"There's a shark in the pool!" screeched Anxious Andrew.

"There's a shark in the pool!" howled Rude Ralph.

Everyone was screaming and shouting and struggling to get out.

The only one left in the pool was Henry.

Shark!

Horrid Henry forgot there were no sharks in swimming pools.

Horrid Henry forgot *he'd* started the shark rumour.

Horrid Henry forgot he couldn't swim.

All he knew was that he was alone in the pool – with a shark!

Horrid Henry swam for his life.

Shaking and quaking, splashing and
crashing, he torpedoed his way to the
side of the pool and scrambled out.
He gasped and panted. Thank goodness.
Safe at last! He'd never ever go
swimming again.

"Five metres!" bellowed Soggy Sid.

"You've all failed your badges today, except for – Henry!"

"Waaaaaaahhhhhh!" wailed the other children.

"Whoopee!" screamed Henry. "Olympics, here I come!"

4

HORRID HENRY
AND THE
MUMMY'S CURSE

Tiptoe. Tiptoe. Tiptoe.

Horrid Henry crept down the hall.
The coast was clear. Mum and Dad were
in the garden, and Peter was playing at
Tidy Ted's.

Tee hee, thought Henry, then darted
into Perfect Peter's room and shut the
door.

There it was. Sitting unopened on
Peter's shelf. The grossest, yuckiest, most
stomach-curdling kit Henry had ever
seen. A brand-new, deluxe "Curse of the
Mummy" kit, complete with a plastic
body to mummify, mummy-wrapping

gauze, curse book, amulets and, best of all, removable mummy organs to put in a canopic jar. Peter had won it at the "Meet a Real Mummy" exhibition at the museum, but he'd never even played with it once.

Of course, Henry wasn't allowed into Peter's bedroom without permission. He was also not allowed to play with Peter's toys. This was so unfair, Henry could hardly believe it. True, he wouldn't let Peter touch his Boom-Boom Basher, his Goo-Shooter, or his Dungeon Drink kit. In fact, since Henry refused to share *any*

68

of his toys with Peter, Mum had forbidden Henry to play with any of Peter's toys – or else.

Henry didn't care – Perfect Peter had boring baby toys – until, that is, he brought home the mummy kit. Henry had ached to play with it. And now was his chance.

Horrid Henry tore off the wrapping, and opened the box.

WOW! So gross! Henry felt a delicious shiver. He loved mummies. What could be more thrilling than looking at an ancient, wrapped-up DEAD body? Even a pretend one was wonderful. And now he had hours of fun ahead of him.

Pitter-patter! Pitter-patter! Pitter-patter!

Oh help, someone was coming up the stairs! Horrid Henry shoved the mummy kit behind him as Peter's bedroom door swung open and Perfect Peter strolled in.

"Out of my way, worm!" shouted
Henry.

Perfect Peter slunk off. Then he
stopped.

"Wait a minute," he said. "You're in *my*
room! You can't order me out of my own
room!"

"Oh yeah?" blustered Henry.

"Yeah!" said Peter.

"You're supposed to be at Ted's," said
Henry, trying to distract him.

"He got sick," said Peter. He stepped
closer. "And you're playing with my kit!
You're not allowed to play with any of

my things! Mum said so! I'm going to tell her right now!"

Uh oh. If Peter told on him Henry would be in big trouble. Very big trouble. Henry had to save himself, fast. He had two choices. He could leap on Peter and throttle him. Or he could use weasel words.

"I wasn't playing with it," said Henry smoothly. "I was trying to protect you."

"No you weren't," said Peter. "I'm telling."

"I was, too," said Henry. "I was trying to protect you from the Mummy's Curse."

Perfect Peter headed for the door. Then he stopped.

"What curse?" said Peter.

"The curse which turns people into mummies!" said Henry desperately.

"There's no such thing," said Peter.

"Wanna bet?" said Henry. "Everyone knows about the mummy's curse! They take on the shape of someone familiar but really, they're mummies! They could be your cat—"

"Fluffy?" said Peter. "Fluffy, a mummy?"

Henry looked at fat Fluffy snoring peacefully on a cushion.

"Even Fluffy," said Henry. "Or Dad. Or Me. Or you."

"I'm not a mummy," said Peter.

"Or even—" Henry paused melo-dramatically and then whispered, "Mum."

"Mum, a mummy?" gasped Peter.

"Yup," said Henry. "But don't worry. You help me draw some Eyes of Horus. They'll protect us against . . . her."

"She's not a mummy," said Peter.

"That's what she wants us to think," whispered Henry. "It's all here in the Mummy curse book." He waved the book in front of Peter. "Don't you think the mummy on the cover resembles you-know-who?"

"No," said Peter.

"Watch," said Horrid Henry. He grabbed a pencil.

"Don't draw on a book!" squeaked
Peter.

Henry ignored him and drew glasses
on the mummy.

"How about now?" he asked.

Peter stared. Was it his imagination or
did the mummy look a little familiar?

"I don't believe you," said Peter. "I'm
going straight down to ask Mum."

"But that's the worst thing you could
do!" shouted Henry.

"I don't care," said Peter. Down he went.

Henry was sunk. Mum would probably cancel his birthday party when Peter blabbed. And he'd never even had a chance to play with the mummy kit! It was so unfair.

Mum was reading on the sofa.

"Mum," said Peter, "Henry says you're a mummy."

Mum looked puzzled.

"Of course I'm a mummy," she said.

"What?" said Peter.

"I'm your mummy," said Mum, with a smile.

Peter took a step back.

"I don't want you to be a mummy," said Peter.

"But I am one," said Mum. "Now come and give me a hug."

"No!" said Peter.

"Let me wrap my arms around you," said Mum.

"NO WRAPPING!" squealed Peter. "I want my mummy!"

"But I'm your mummy," said Mum.

"I know!" squeaked Peter. "Keep away, you . . . Mummy!"

Perfect Peter staggered up the stairs to Henry.

"It's true," he gasped. "She said she was a mummy."

"She did?" said Henry.

"Yes," said Peter. "What are we going to do?"

"Don't worry, Peter," said Henry. "We can free her from the curse."

"How?" breathed Peter.

Horrid Henry pretended to consult the curse book.

"First we must sacrifice to the Egyptian gods Osiris and Hroth," said Henry.

"Sacrifice?" said Peter.

"They like cat guts, and stuff like that," said Henry.

"No!" squealed Peter. "Not . . . Fluffy!"

"However," said Henry, leafing through the curse book, "marbles are also acceptable as an offering."

Perfect Peter ran to his toybox and scooped up a handful of marbles.

"Now fetch me some loo roll," added Henry.

"Loo roll?" said Peter.

"Do not question the priest of Anubis!" shrieked Henry.

Perfect Peter fetched the loo roll.

"We must wrap Fluffy in the sacred bandages," said Henry. "He will be our messenger between this world and the next."

"Meoww," said Fluffy, as he was wrapped from head to tail in loo paper.

"Now you," said Henry.

"Me?" squeaked Peter.

"Yes," said Henry. "Do you want to free Mum from the mummy's curse?"

Peter nodded.

"Then you must stand still and be quiet for thirty minutes," said Henry. That should give him plenty of time to have a go with the mummy kit.

He started wrapping Peter. Round and round and round and round went the loo roll until Peter was tightly trussed from head to toe.

Henry stepped back to admire his work. Goodness, he was a brilliant mummy-maker! Maybe that's what he should be when he grew up. Henry, the Mummy-Maker. Henry, World's Finest Mummy-Maker. Henry, Mummy-Maker to the Stars. Yes, it certainly had a ring to it.

"You're a fine-looking mummy, Peter," said Henry. "I'm sure you'll be made very welcome in the next world."

"Huuunh?"said Peter.

"Silence!"ordered Henry. "Don't move. Now I must utter the sacred spell. By the powers of Horus, Morus, Borus and Stegosaurus," intoned Henry, making up all the Egyptian sounding names he could.

"Stegosaurus?" mumbled Peter.

"Whatever!" snapped Henry. "I call on the scarab! I call on Isis! Free Fluffy from the mummy's curse. Free Peter from the mummy's curse. Free Mum from the mummy's curse. Free— "

"What on earth is going on in here?" shrieked Mum, bursting through the door. "You horrid boy! What have you done to Peter? And what have you done to poor Fluffy?"

81

"Meoww," yowled Fluffy.

"Mummy!" squealed Perfect Peter.

Eowww, gross! thought Horrid Henry, opening up the plastic mummy body and placing the organs in the canopic jar.

The bad news was that Henry had been banned from watching TV for a week. The good news was that Perfect Peter had said he never wanted to see that horrible mummy kit again.

HORRID HENRY BOOKS

Horrid Henry
Horrid Henry and the Secret Club
Horrid Henry Tricks the Tooth Fairy
Horrid Henry's Nits
Horrid Henry Gets Rich Quick
Horrid Henry's Haunted House
Horrid Henry and the Mummy's Curse
Horrid Henry's Revenge
Horrid Henry and the Bogey Babysitter
Horrid Henry's Stinkbomb
Horrid Henry's Underpants
Horrid Henry Meets the Queen
Horrid Henry and the Mega-Mean Time Machine
Horrid Henry and the Football Fiend
Horrid Henry's Christmas Cracker
Horrid Henry and the Abominable Snowman
Horrid Henry Robs the Bank

Colour books

Horrid Henry's Big Bad Book
Horrid Henry's Wicked Ways
Horrid Henry's Evil Enemies
Horrid Henry Rules the World

Joke Books

Horrid Henry's Joke Book
Horrid Henry's Jolly Joke Book
Horrid Henry's Mighty Joke Book

Activity Books

Horrid Henry's Brainbusters
Horrid Henry's Headscratchers
Horrid Henry's Mindbenders
Horrid Henry's Colouring Book
Horrid Henry's Puzzle Book
Horrid Henry's Sticker Book
Horrid Henry's Crazy Crosswords
Horrid Henry's Mad Mazes
Horrid Henry's Wicked Wordsearches

Horrid Henry is also available on audio CD and digital download, all read by Miranda Richardson.

"A hoot from beginning to end . . . As always, Miranda Richardson's delivery is perfection and the manic music is a delight."
Daily Express

"Long may this dreadful boy continue to terrorise all who know him. He's a nightmare, but so entertaining . . . Miranda Richardson's spirited reading is accompanied by a brilliant music soundtrack – they make a noisy and fun-filled duo."
Parents' Guide

Also by Francesca Simon

HORRID HENRY

Henry is dragged to dancing class against his will; vies with Moody Margaret to make the yuckiest Glop, goes camping in France and tries to be good like Perfect Peter – but not for long.

HORRID HENRY

AND THE SECRET CLUB

Horrid Henry gets an injection, torments
his little brother Perfect Peter, creates
havoc at his own birthday party, and plans
sweet revenge when Moody Margaret
won't let him into her Secret Club.

HORRID HENRY
TRICKS THE TOOTH FAIRY

(Originally published as
Horrid Henry and the Tooth Fairy)

Horrid Henry tries to trick the Tooth
Fairy into giving him more money, sends
Moody Margaret packing, causes his
teachers to run screaming from school,
and single-handedly wrecks a wedding.

HORRID HENRY'S
NITS

Scratch. Scratch. Scratch. Horrid Henry has nits – and he's on a mission to give them to everyone else too. After that, he can turn his attention to wrecking the school trip, ruining his parents' dinner party, and terrifying Perfect Peter.

HORRID HENRY'S
HAUNTED HOUSE

Horrid Henry slugs it out with Perfect
Peter over the remote control, stays in a
haunted house and gets a nasty shock,
discovers where X marks the spot in
the hidden treasure competition and
stars on TV.

HORRID HENRY
GETS RICH QUICK

(Originally published as
Horrid Henry Strikes It Rich)

Horrid Henry tries to sell off Perfect
Peter and get rich, makes sure he gets
the presents he wants for Christmas,
sabotages Sports Day at school – and
runs away from home.

HORRID HENRY'S
REVENGE

Horrid Henry accompanies his father
to the office, hacks into his parent's
computer, meets the Demon Dinner
Lady and plans the ultimate revenge on
Perfect Peter.

HORRID HENRY
AND THE
BOGEY BABYSITTER

Horrid Henry encounters the babysitter from hell, traumatizes his parents on a car journey, goes trick or treating at Hallowe'en, and invades Moody Margaret's Secret Club.

Helping Hercules

Who was Orpheus and why did he play such sad music? Why does Atlas have the weight of the world on his shoulders? And how did the hideous Medusa eventually lose her head?

Susan is just a normal school girl – bored with homework, chores, and her parents constantly nagging her – until one day she finds the old Greek coin given to her by her Uncle Martin. Suddenly history lessons take on a whole new meaning as Susan travels through time to join forces with the heroes and villains of Ancient Greece!

In these pacey, action packed stories, Greek myths and legends come alive as Susan helps her new old world friends in a variety of ways – but just how does she mimic Midas and persuade Paris?